STAR ATTACK!

L.A. COURTENAY

ILLUSTRATED BY
JAMES DAVIES

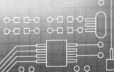

STONE ARCH BOOKS
a capstone imprint

Space Penguins books are published by Stone Arch Books
A Capstone Imprint
1710 Roe Crest Drive
North Mankato, Minnesota 56003
www.capstoneyoungreaders.com

First published by Stripes Publishing Ltd.
1 The Coda Centre
189 Munster Road
London SW6 6AW

Library of Congress Cataloging-in-Publication Data is
available on the Library of Congress website.

ISBN: 978-1-4342-9784-6 (library binding)
ISBN: 978-1-4342-9788-4 (paperback)
ISBN: 978-1-4965-0204-9 (eBook PDF)

Summary: When the crew of the *Tunafish* pick up a distress
signal from a spaceship, there's snow time to lose. But the
Tunafish's daring rescue is canned when the vessel runs into
its own trouble. What's been luring spaceships to their doom?

Printed in China.
092014   008472RRDS15

TABLE OF CONTENTS

MEET THE SPACE PENGUINS...

CAPTAIN:
James T. Krill
Emperor penguin
Height: 3 ft. 7 in.
Looks: yellow ear patches and noble bearing
Likes: swordfish minus the sword
Lab Test Results: showed leadership qualities in fish challenge
Guaranteed to: keep calm in a crisis

FIRST MATE (ONCE UPON A TIME):
Beaky Wader, now known as Dark Wader
Emperor penguin
Height: 4 ft.
Looks: yellow ear patches and evil laugh
Likes: prawn pizza
Lab Test Results: cheated at every challenge
Guaranteed to: cause trouble

PILOT (WITH NO SENSE OF DIRECTION):

Rocky Waddle
Rockhopper penguin
Height: 1 ft. 6 in.
Looks: long yellow eyebrows
Likes: mackerel ice cream
Lab Test Results: fastest slider in toboggan challenge
Guaranteed to: speed through an asteroid belt while reading charts upside down

SECURITY OFFICER AND HEAD CHEF:

Fuzz Allgrin
Little Blue penguin
Height: 1 ft. 1 in.
Looks: small with fuzzy blue feathers
Likes: fish sticks in cream and truffle sauce
Lab Test Results: showed creativity and aggression in ice-carving challenge
Guaranteed to: defend ship, crew, and kitchen with his life

SHIP'S ENGINEER:

Splash Gordon
King penguin
Height: 3 ft. 1 in.
Looks: orange ears and chest markings
Likes: squid
Lab Test Results: solved ice-cube challenge in under four seconds
Guaranteed to: fix anything

LOADING...

Welcome aboard the spaceship *Tunafish*. This is your Intergalactic Computer Engine speaking. You can call me ICEcube for short.

I'm here to guide the *Tunafish* through the universe, scan the galaxy for meteor storms, and spot any black holes. My penguin crew would have flapped their last flap years ago if it wasn't for me.

Penguin crew? Yep! Penguins are perfect for space missions. They're good at swimming (being in space is a lot like swimming), will work for fish, and are untroubled by temperatures near zero.

But why are these penguins in space? You'll have to ask NASA about that. Their finest scientists started a top-secret mission to send penguins farther and faster than any creature had gone before. They designed the spaceship *Tunafish* for all their needs. But the spaceship disappeared. Everyone thought that the mission had simply been a failure. Little did they know that the *Tunafish* and its penguin crew had just been sucked through a wormhole into Deep Space.

My database suggests that the best word for this is: whoops!

So now these penguins are traveling in search of a nice planet to call home. In the course of their quest, they've become intergalactic heroes. They've saved the cat race of Miaow from certain death on the planet Woofbark. They've even destroyed a large pair of frozen pants that was endangering space traffic on the tiny planet of Bum. They wouldn't have been so successful if it weren't for me, of course. Impressed?

There were five penguins to begin with, but the first mate, Beaky Wader, disappeared from the *Tunafish* three years ago after a nasty argument about who was going to be captain. The words "You haven't seen the last of me" echoed around the spaceship for days. Good riddance, I say. Beaky Wader was Trouble with a capital Fish.

And now — well, now they're still looking for the perfect penguin planet to call home. We'll probably be rescuing things as we go along, so I know you're as excited as I am to be here. Fasten your seatbelt and have a sardine. I would say that you are in safe hands, but penguins only have flippers.

Five. Four. Three. Two. One . . .

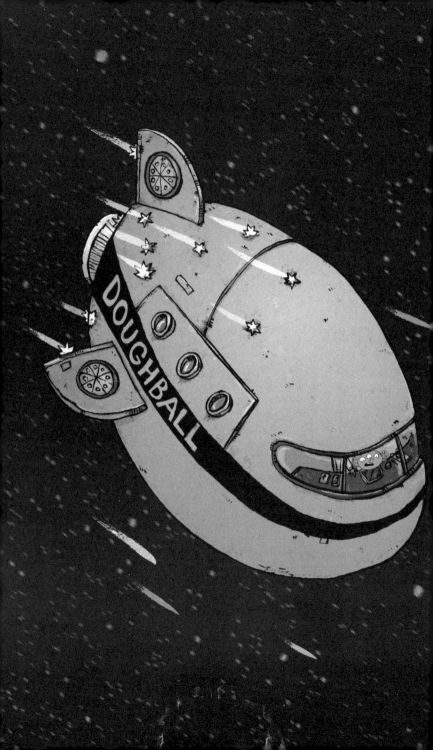

BOBBY CHEESE
HAS A BAD DAY

"Help!" bawled Bobby Cheese.

The commander of the intergalactic pizza-delivery spaceship, the *Doughball*, was zooming toward certain death. A crazy-looking spacecraft had appeared out of nowhere, driving him off-course in a blaze of gunfire.

"Awaiting instruction," said the *Doughball's* computer.

"I *am* instructing you!" yelled Bobby Cheese. "Help me!"

He thumped all the buttons on the *Doughball*'s shaking control panel in a panic. Bobby Cheese was a six-armed alien from the planet Bo-Ki, but even so, two thousand buttons took a long time to thump.

"Awaiting instruction," said the computer again. "Chill out, Cheese," it added.

"Don't tell me to chill out!" Bobby Cheese wailed. "We're hopelessly out of control!"

Stars shot past the *Doughball*'s windows at weird angles. Bobby Cheese moaned. He didn't know if he was upside down or right side up.

"Awaiting instruction," said the computer for the third time.

"You're useless!" cried Bobby Cheese. "We've got nearly a thousand pizzas flying around in the back. They'll be ruined. We'll be picking mozzarella out of the fuselage for weeks unless we get this ship back under control!"

"We'll be picking you out of the fuselage as well," the computer said helpfully.

"Quit the small talk and get me out of here," Bobby Cheese yelled. "Do you have any idea who's attacking us?"

The computer was quiet for a second. "The attack is by Squid-G fighters," it said at last.

"Squidgy what?"

"Squid-G fighters. Spacecrafts with considerable firepower and a strong fishy smell."

"But why are they attacking me?" shrieked Bobby Cheese.

"For fun?" suggested the computer.

The *Doughball* spun faster. Its nose dipped farther. The stars outside grew stranger. Bobby Cheese glanced at a tattered poster stuck on the wall. The poster showed four penguins posing beside a fish-shaped spacecraft.

"Only the heroic astronauts of the *Tunafish* can help me now," he said. "We have to contact them!"

"But they're just penguins," said the computer. "Are you sure you want to put your life into the flippers of four flightless fowl?"

"They're not just penguins!" cried Bobby Cheese. "They're space-fighting heroes! If

I haven't died by the time they get here, remind me to get their autographs!"

The strange stars suddenly disappeared from view altogether as the spinning *Doughball* plunged into a bank of mist. Bobby Cheese typed a shaky distress call to the spaceship *Tunafish* and pressed send. Squinting desperately through the windshield, his eyes widened at the sight of a gigantic five-pointed star looming ahead of him.

"What's that? Is it a planet?"

"Planets don't have pointy parts. That's a space station," reported the computer.

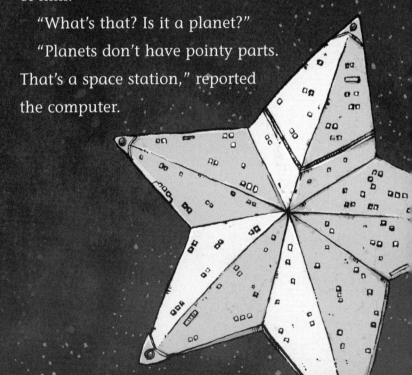

The air filled with a humming sound. Bobby Cheese groaned and pressed his hands to as many of his ears as he could reach. It was all over. The *Doughball* was doomed.

Where was the *Tunafish* in his hour of greatest need?

CHAPTER TWO

SMELLY SOCKS

The problem with Deep Space is that it is extremely Deep. And Spacious. And at that particular moment, the spaceship *Tunafish* was a hundred million light-years away.

The Space Penguins had just sorted out an army of invading purple blobs on the planet Tentakle. After chilling in the freezing-fog room (the penguin version of a steam room), they were now back at work and on their way to — well, anywhere that looked nice, really.

"Rocky," said Captain Krill, addressing his pilot. "Tell me again exactly how far we've traveled since our rescue mission on the planet Tentakle."

"Two hundred thousand light-years, Captain," Rocky repeated.

Captain James T. Krill had a frown on his face. He placed his flippers behind his sleek black back and stared at his large black feet. "I thought we'd gone at least a hundred light-years more," he said. "Are you sure?"

Rocky Waddle was a pretty good pilot but his navigating could sometimes be a few million miles off — mainly because his eyebrows covered his eyes. Rockhopper penguins have *very* big eyebrows.

"I'm one hundred percent sure it's two hundred thousand light-years, Captain," Rocky promised. He checked the engine screens. "Engine one is firing on all cylinders. Engines two and three, likewise. Aha! What's this?"

He twiddled a knob and zoomed in on one of the engine sections. A red light was flashing. "There's a problem with engine four, Captain," said Rocky. He tapped the screen with his flipper. "Something's jamming it."

A small, fluffy blue penguin poked his head out of a door marked DO NOT ENTER THE KITCHEN ON PAIN OF PECKING UNLESS FUZZ SAYS IT'S OK.

"It's not a Tentakle blob, is it?" asked Fuzz Allgrin, Security Officer and Head Chef aboard the *Tunafish*. There was a fierce expression in his tiny black eyes and a terrifying knife gleamed in one of his flippers. "I was about to cook one for dinner, but it escaped through a ventilation hatch."

Captain Krill wrinkled his beak. "We're having a Tentakle blob for dinner?"

Fuzz glared. "I don't know if you've noticed, Captain, but decent fish is hard to come by in space. Tentakle blobs may taste like feet, but at least they have a texture like octopus."

"It's not a Tentakle blob," said Rocky. "It's

sort of long, and yellowish, and feathery-looking . . . Oh, sorry, no. That's my eyebrow. So what's jamming engine four, ICEcube?"

"Species identification in engine four: Tentakle blob. One of two hundred and thirty-three presently aboard the *Tunafish*, acquired for food during our recent mission on the planet Tentakle," said ICEcube at once. "Known for their lack of intelligence, vibrant purple color, rubbery texture, and powerful smell of socks."

"We know that," said Rocky with a shudder.

A door hissed open and a large King penguin in a huge pair of goggles bustled in, wiping his flippers on his tummy and leaving long oily smears on his feathers. It was the ship's engineer, Splash Gordon.

"Turn engine four to full," said Splash. He removed his goggles with a twang. "The blob will be blasted out in one point four seconds. I've adjusted the heat regulator on the engine."

"Good advice, Splash," said Captain Krill. "Rocky, proceed as Splash suggests."

Rocky flipped engine four to full. There was a blast of heat and a sizzling noise. A hot sock smell filled the air. One point four seconds later, the crew felt the *Tunafish* leap forward.

"Back to full cruising speed, Captain,"

Rocky confirmed, settling back into his pilot's chair.

"Distress signal just in, Captain," said ICEcube. "Attack by Squid-G fighters. I need your help. Free pizzas if you get here quick."

"Free pizzas?" said Splash.

"Squid-G? Sounds fishy," said Captain Krill.

Rocky slapped the arms of his chair with his flippers and roared with laughter. "Good one, Captain!" he said. "Squid! Sounds fishy!"

"This is no time for jokes," said Captain Krill with a frown. "Rocky, download the coordinates of the stricken ship. We must fly to its aid immediately. One for all and all for fish. Warp speed, right away!"

CHAPTER THREE

WARP SPEED WHIFF

Rocky hit warp speed faster than you can say seatbelts.

As the *Tunafish* zapped through a hundred million light-years in the blink of an eye, the penguins were all tossed around. Captain Krill struggled to his feet. Splash unpeeled himself from the ceiling.

"You total squid-head, Rocky," shouted Fuzz from beneath a pile of twitching Tentakle blobs. "We didn't have time to fasten our seatbelts. It stinks under here!"

"The captain said right away!" Rocky said, laughing uncontrollably.

Captain Krill felt his way back to the commander's chair as Fuzz and Splash chased the blobs back into the kitchen and shut the door. The smell improved.

"So where are the Squid-G fighters that were attacking the spaceship in distress?" Captain Krill asked when his brain had stopped spinning. He peered through the *Tunafish*'s windshield at the misty patch of space they'd landed in.

"No one's out there," complained Fuzz. "Typical. You drop everything, get covered in blobs and then —"

"Wait!" Captain Krill interrupted. "What's that?"

Looming in the mist was a ginormous structure, hanging in the sky like a Christmas star. It was fat and silvery and covered in thousands of tiny windows that blinked with light. Dazzling beams shot from its five tips. It was so vast that the penguins had trouble seeing all of it.

The *Tunafish* took an unexpected nosedive, squashing the crew to the backs of their seats. With perfect timing, the Tentakle blobs tumbled back through the kitchen door, shot across the bridge, and splatted onto the windshield. The stench was terrible.

"Now I'm angry," said Fuzz.

"Like you weren't angry before?" said Rocky.

"What's going on, ICEcube?" asked Captain Krill.

"We are caught in the traction beam of a large star-shaped space station," ICEcube replied.

"Any sign of the spacecraft we're supposed to be helping?" asked Rocky.

"Nope," said Fuzz.

"Maybe the space station gobbled it up?"
Splash suggested.

There was a strange humming sound.
Captain Krill could feel his yellow ear
patches shriveling up. "I think that's exactly
what it did," he said, shouting over the
noise. "And it looks as though it's about to
gobble us too! Hold on tight!"

The crew of the *Tunafish* couldn't see it, but right in front of their blob-covered windshield, one of the starfish arms on the gigantic space station was lifting up. Up, up, up it went, opening like the beak of a huge silver pelican. Quick as a flash, the *Tunafish* was sucked inside.

It landed with a crunch. The blobs slithered off the *Tunafish*'s windshield and flopped into the penguins' laps. Everyone blinked, dazzled by the blinding white light around them.

They had arrived in some kind of spaceport. Several shiny starships were parked nearby. It was huge and airy and extremely cold.

"Hopping halibuts," said Fuzz. He stood on his chair to get a better view. "Check this place out! It looks like it's been carved from a huge block of . . . What's that stuff called? You know, the stuff that's cold? And white?

And rhymes with mice? We used to sit on it all day in the zoo."

The others stared back blankly.

"It's been a long time since we were on Earth," said Captain Krill.

"Polystyrene?" Rocky suggested.

"Ice," said Splash at the same time.

"That's the stuff!" said Fuzz. "Ice!"

"Now I remember it!" said Rocky.

"I used ice cubes to solve my first ever math problem," said Splash.

"These are exciting observations, crew," said Captain Krill. "But let's not forget our mission here. The creature who sent us the distress signal is somewhere on this space station. And I'm guessing that's his ship."

A rusty spacecraft was parked right in front of the *Tunafish*. It looked small and out of place among the gleaming starships and white icy walls. A wobbly picture of a pizza was painted on its wings and tail fin, and it had the word *DOUGHBALL* on both sides. Piles of empty pizza boxes lay scattered around the spacecraft's grubby landing gear.

"Don't look now," said Rocky, "but someone's noticed we've arrived."

Hundreds of strange-looking silver robots were moving rapidly toward the *Tunafish*. Their bodies gleamed and their eyes flashed as their moving metal parts clonked loudly on the ice.

CHAPTER FOUR

BATTLE FOR SURVIVAL

"Something about those guys makes me nervous," said Rocky, gazing out of the windshield at the clonking silver robots.

"Wuss," Fuzz said.

"Interesting," said Splash. "Apart from their mechanical and electronic specifications, their overlapping plate armor, their visible circuit boards, and their flashing red LED eyes, they look exactly like leopard seals."

"Are you saying that we're looking at

robot versions of the greatest predator of penguins?" said Rocky in shock.

"Yep," said Splash.

Fuzz started practicing his fight moves, punching the air with his little flippers and muttering things under his breath like, "Take that, you blubbering bully! You mechanized mollusk! And that! And that!"

The robot seals were getting closer. *CLONK. CLONK. CLONK.*

"Arm yourselves, crew," Captain Krill commanded. "We may have a battle on our flippers. Let's show those seals what we're made of!"

"About one hundred pounds of blubber," said Splash. "If you add everyone up."

"ICEcube?" said Captain Krill. "What weapons have we got that are fully charged and ready for fighting?"

CLONK. CLONK. CLONK.

"Pulse pistols: three," said ICEcube.

"Rocket rifles: two. Bazooka-blammers: one. Zap-o-blasters: two. Stun guns: three. Space cannon: one."

"Bring it on!" shouted Fuzz.

The penguins grabbed their weapons as the door of the *Tunafish* blasted open. They were dazzled by the fierce red beams of a hundred robotic seal eyes.

"All for one and one for fish!" roared the captain. "Attack!"

He fired a pulse pistol at the nearest robot seal. *PYOW!* Little pieces of robot rained down on the fighting heroes.

Splash took aim with a zap-o-blaster.

KABOOM!

Two more robot seals stumbled and fell, wires dangling uselessly from their metal bodies.

"Let me at 'em! Let me unleash the bazooka-blammer!" Fuzz yelled.

BLLLAAAMMM!

The bazooka-blammer made more noise than the zap-o-blaster and the pulse pistol put together. Fuzz fell over with the force of it. It put four more robot seals out of action and made a large hole in the wall of the

Tunafish. But it wasn't enough. The silver fighting machines kept coming.

"My stun gun isn't working," Rocky shouted as he jumped and spun and fought. "It's just making a boop noise!"

"Stun guns only work on living things, Rocky," Splash said, dodging an oncoming seal. *KABOOM!* His zap-o-blaster was running dangerously low on power.

Rocky wasn't listening. He peered down his stun-gun barrel. "Maybe I just need to press this button here. It's worth a —"

BOOP. The rockhopper pilot slid to the floor.

"We're a penguin down, Captain!" Fuzz shouted. "Rocky just knocked himself out with his own stun gun!"

Nearly all their weapons were out of power and ammunition. The only thing left was the space cannon, but it would blow the penguins sky-high along with the robots. In desperation, Captain Krill picked a Tentakle blob off the floor and hurled it. *SPLAT!* A silver monster staggered and tipped sideways with the nasty smell of sock.

"Right in the circuit board!" shouted Splash. "Woohoo!"

It was amazing what a flipperful of blobs could do. *SPLAT! SPLAT! SPLAT!* A dozen robot seals were blobbed, and then a dozen more. When the blobs ran out, the penguins used things from the *Tunafish*'s food stores. An old lump of frozen haddock. *CHONK!* Tins of sprats in squid-ink sauce. *WHANG!* Dried flying disks of salted cod. *WHEE!*

"Ninja penguin!" screamed Fuzz, whirling his flippers like blades.

"What's going on?" mumbled Rocky as he woke up.

There were fish everywhere. On the ceiling, in the control panels. A handful of frozen shrimp started cooking in the light fittings, filling the *Tunafish* with wonderful smells. But all the penguin power aboard that spaceship was no match for the robot army. There were too many of them.

"If you eat me, you'll get the worst stomachache of your measly mechanical life!" Fuzz roared as a robot carried him off the ship. Four more seized Captain Krill. Three grabbed Splash. Two more hefted Rocky over their heads. The four penguins were dumped onto the ice outside.

They struggled to their feet as a huge, black, penguin-shaped robot came gliding toward them.

"Well, if it isn't my old penguin friends," it said.

CHAPTER FIVE

DARK WADER

It looked like Beaky Wader, the old first mate of the *Tunafish*, who had vanished from the spaceship three years earlier. And yet at the same time, it didn't look like Beaky at all.

"That's impossible!" said Fuzz.

"That's incredible!" said Rocky.

"That's very technologically advanced," said Splash.

The large armor-plated penguin raised a pair of glittery metal eyebrows at the captain. "Anything you'd like to add?"

"Hello Beaky," said Captain Krill coolly.

"I call myself Dark these days," said Beaky Wader. "Dark Wader. Hello, Krill. It's 'ice' to see you." He laughed at his own joke. "Ha-ha-ha! I'm even more brilliant than I thought!"

"You'll forgive me if I don't ask you aboard for a fish supper, Beaky," said the captain with a stern face. But —"

"You never did have a sense of humor,

Krill," Beaky interrupted. "And the name's Dark. As in: how your future looks if you keep calling me Beaky."

Fuzz pointed to the empty pizza boxes lying beside the rusty *Doughball*. "Did you steal those pizzas?" he asked.

"Of course I did," said Beaky. "Decent pizzas don't grow on trees. And even if they did, trees don't grow in space."

"What have you done with the crew?" demanded Captain Krill. "It's against intergalactic regulations to —"

"I can't hear you," said Beaky. "La la la. Boring. Like everything you ever say, Krill."

Splash looked at Beaky's shiny black armor, his gleaming helmet, and his shiny silver wheels. "Loving the outfit, Beaky," he said. "I mean, Dark."

Beaky Wader brushed a speck of dust off his blinking electronic chest. "Good, isn't it?" he said with a smirk.

"You look like a remote-control trash can," said Fuzz.

Beaky Wader glared. He clapped his armored flippers with an ear-piercing clang. "Masher?" he said to the nearest robot seal. "Escort our guests. Cruncher?" he said to the second nearest. "Make sure no one in the back gets lost."

A small, red, spiny creature suddenly skidded into view and crashed hard against the *Tunafish*'s landing gear, making the penguins jump.

"Sorry I'm late," said the creature. It looked like a crab with a tail and an extra pairs of eyes on the tips of its claws. "What did I miss?"

"This is Crabba," said Dark Wader. "He is mean, vicious, untrustworthy, venomous, highly dangerous, and utterly loyal to me."

Crabba scuttled up Dark Wader's armored body and sat on his shoulder. He gazed at the Space Penguins with interest. "I am pretty venomous, yeah," he said. "It's all in the claws. But I'll only pinch you if you annoy me."

"Our guests are tired and in need of rest and refreshment, Crabba," said Dark Wader. "Shall we escort them to their sleeping pods?"

"What have you done with the crew of the *Doughball*?" Captain Krill repeated stubbornly, but Dark Wader ignored him.

Masher and Cruncher snapped their jaws as the *Tunafish* crew waddled after their gliding host as speedily as they could. Captain Krill's beak was already icing up. The freezing wind howling around the space station was as cold as the Antarctic. The Space Penguins started almost enjoying the experience.

"I wish you'd turn the temperature up, boss," Crabba said.

"Crabba cannot understand the beauty of snow and ice," said Dark Wader. "He's from somewhere hot." He said the word "hot" like it was a bad-tasting kipper. "But you can, can't you, my friends? It's in our blood. Our bones."

"Beaky's a walking advertisement for motorized components," Splash whispered to Captain Krill. "I've never seen such smooth action from an aquatic bird."

Everywhere the penguins looked, robot seals were watching them with unblinking red eyes. What had happened to their old space-mate in the three years since they had last seen him? Why was Beaky now a robot living on a star-shaped space station with an army of metal guards?

"We need to escape, Captain," whispered Fuzz as they waddled along. "I've got a really bad feeling about Beaky and his plans."

"Too many robot seals watching, Fuzz," replied Captain Krill quietly. "Escaping will have to wait. And besides, we've got to rescue the crew of the *Doughball*."

They stopped in front of a large ice hole carved into the wall, marked SLEEPING PODS.

"It's late," said Dark Wader. "I never sleep, but you flesh-and-blood intergalactic heroes will need

SLEEPING PODS

a little snooze." He sneered at the word "heroes." "We shall part until the morning, when I have something to discuss with you, perhaps over a pizza breakfast. Don't try any heroics. I can assure you, they will end badly."

Masher and Cruncher pushed the penguins into the ice hole. Suddenly they

were slipping and sliding through a tunnel. The air rushed over their sleek feathers like silk. It was fantastic! It was fabulous! It was like the world's best waterslide, only drier and a whole bunch colder.

After a full two minutes of twisting tunnels, the breathless penguins tumbled head-over-flippers out of the end of the

tunnel and landed with a mighty splash in a deep blue ice pool.

"This is our sleeping pod? WAHOO!" shouted Rocky, bobbing to the surface. He shook his eyebrows, spraying droplets of ice-cold water everywhere.

"Check this place out," Fuzz said with awe.

The penguins sprang from the water and landed on the craggy white shoreline of the pool. They stared at their surroundings.

Four comfortable sleeping platforms were carved into the rock in one corner, while a frozen fish vending machine stood in another. There was an ice slide curving around the walls and ending in the pool.

"I'm so trying that," said Rocky, scrambling up the snow steps that led to the top and launching himself down the slide.

"Do I see mackerel?" said Splash, gazing at the vending machine.

"I haven't had mackerel in years," said Fuzz.

Captain Krill pressed the button on the vending machine. It made a whumping noise and a top drawer flew open, sending an arc of spring-loaded mackerel straight into the waiting penguins' beaks. *PING. PING. PING.*

"WAHOOOOO!" screamed Rocky as he landed in the pool again.

"It's awesome here!" said Fuzz.

"Why is Beaky being so nice to us?" Captain Krill mused. "I don't trust him. That pizza spaceship crew is on this space station somewhere, and they need us. Let's not lose sight of that. We'll escape as soon as we can."

No one noticed the tiny jellyfish-shaped robot creeping through a crack in the wall and attaching itself to the ceiling. A miniature lens shot out of its body and focused on the penguins below.

At once, a stream of words and pictures were fed back to a large computer in the space station's control room. Dark Wader tapped his flippers together thoughtfully as he watched and listened.

CHAPTER SIX

THE GREAT ICE DECK

The next morning, an icy splash of water woke the penguins. Two enormous robot seals had zoomed through the ice tunnel door and landed with a sploosh in the pool.

"I'm guessing they have waterproof circuitry," said Splash.

"No kidding, fish brains," said Fuzz.

The seals leaped ashore and herded the penguins toward another doorway in the wall marked GREAT ICE DECK.

The new ice slide was even twistier than

the last one, and the penguins enjoyed the ride. The little jellyfish-shaped spy-cam followed a short distance behind them.

"This is almost as much fun as yesterday!" shouted Rocky as they banked steeply around a corner. "The only difference is that yesterday we were sliding away from Wader. Today we're sliding straight toward —"

Flump. The penguin astronauts landed in a heap in the middle of a huge snowdrift, right in the heart of a gigantic deck. Dark Wader, Crabba, fifteen robot seals, and a long table covered in prawn pizzas were waiting for them.

"Help yourselves," said Dark Wader between bites. "They're chilled."

"What do you want, Wader? Why are we here?" demanded Captain Krill. "Where's the crew of the *Doughball*?"

"Patience, Krill. You are too eager. All will

be revealed — in time," said Dark Wader. "But for now I suggest that you eat while you can."

The penguins cautiously nibbled on some cold slices of prawn pizza. It tasted fabulous.

Huge icy walls glittered around them. Lights twinkled among the thousands of deadly-looking icicles that hung from the ceiling. An immense tank of water stood in the middle of the deck, containing something that made loud sloshing noises every few minutes. Rows of shiny silver control buttons lined the walls, marked with different temperatures: CHILLY, COLD, ANTARCTIC, and FOOTBALL FIELD IN DECEMBER.

"You're impressed with my Great Ice Deck, aren't you?" said Dark Wader.

"It's a big white room," said Rocky.

Dark Wader frowned in annoyance. "It's

the heart of my vast starfish-shaped space station," he corrected.

Beaky had always been boastful. They might get some useful information about the *Doughball* and its crew if they encouraged him to boast about what he'd been doing. The Space Penguins had used the strategy many times before, usually when trying to trick Fuzz into revealing what he was cooking for dinner.

"What's it been — three years since you left the *Tunafish*?" Captain Krill began. "And you've got your own little space station to show for it. That's nice."

"My *Death Starfish* is not little," said the big pengbot indignantly. "It's vast and unique! I designed and built every last part of it with my own bare flippers."

"Sure you did," said Rocky.

Hot spots of color rose in Dark Wader's

metal cheeks. "Okay, so thousands of RoboSeals did the actual building, but so what? I'm the brains behind the design!"

"No offense," said Splash, "but anyone can build a bunch of mechanized blubber-bins and then order them around. I could, anyway."

"You won't believe the things that I've done since leaving your pathetic sardine can of a spacecraft!" protested Dark Wader.

He was working himself into a tantrum. "I designed that great terror of the skies: the Squid-G fighter!"

There was still no mention of the *Doughball* and its crew.

"Anything else?" said Captain Krill hopefully.

"He gave himself titanium bones, wheels, and waterproof armor," Crabba said from his perch on Dark Wader's shoulder. "He can live in any atmosphere and at any temperature, though he prefers it cold. He doesn't need to eat, drink, or sleep, though he still likes the taste of fish. Although, between you and me, I did all the tricky jobs."

"Under my orders!" said Wader.

"Mildly impressive, Beaky, I admit," said Rocky.

"It's taken me years to get this far, and I've hardly even started," Dark Wader ranted. "So it's *Dark* if you don't mind."

"Sorry, Beaky." Rocky smoothed his eyebrows out of the way. "I'll get the hang of it eventually."

"Shall I poison him, boss?" Crabba offered.

"Tempting, Crabba," said Dark Wader, calming down. "But it will take too long, and I would like to keep things moving. My fellow penguins, before you is the centerpiece of my creation. Ice tunnels lead from here to all points of my *Death Starfish*. We have the control room and engine room in Point One. The jail cells are in Point Two. The spaceport, cargo bays, and hangars holding my spare Squid-G fighters are in Point Three. Point Four holds the laboratories, and Point Five has the kitchens and the Fish Station. Isn't it glorious?"

I need to keep him talking, thought Captain Krill. "What about the *Doughball*?" he asked.

"The *Doughball* no longer exists," the pengbot said impatiently. "We have already eaten most of its cargo, and the fuselage has been stripped down. My RoboSeals are turning what's left of it into another top-of-the-line Squid-G fighter. We'll probably do the same with the *Tunafish*. I recycle all the ships I capture. I'm very eco-friendly."

"And the crew?"

"There was only one of them, Krill. A six-armed creature that claimed to be a pilot. I don't know why you're so worried about it anyway," Dark Wader said in annoyance. "The creature is cooling its heels in the jail cells while I decide what to do with it."

"The jail cells in Point Two?" said the captain.

"Of *course* the jail cells in Point Two!" roared Dark Wader. "Point Two is where the jail cells *are*!"

CHAPTER SEVEN

PENGUIN PARADISE

Fuzz waddled over to the huge tank in the center of the room. "What's in here?" he said, hopping up some steps and peering into the water.

Dark Wader had calmed down again. "My robot killer whale," he said proudly.

A huge creature leaped up from the depths, splashing water everywhere. The penguins glimpsed overlapping scales of black-and-white metal. The thing was gigantic. It thrashed its black-and-white

tail, and it slammed together a set of razor-
sharp steel teeth twice as tall as Fuzz. With
a boom, the whale fell back into the water.
Hundreds of icicles broke away from the
ceiling and plummeted to the ground. The
penguins danced out of the way.

"I don't worry about being spiked these days," said Dark Wader as an icicle shattered on his helmet. "Now that I'm mostly made of metal."

"Why did you build a *killer whale*?" demanded Fuzz. He had just barely escaped a gigantic dagger of ice that had plunged into the ground by his feet.

"Why not?" said Dark Wader. "I'm quite pleased with him."

"You're a *penguin*, Wader!" said Fuzz. "Killer whales eat penguins! You must be insane!"

"I am more than just a penguin now," corrected Dark Wader. "I'm part robot. A mega-penguin. If I want to create high-tech seals and whales that follow my orders, then I will." He grinned evilly. "Now it's time to show you my Fish Station. My living refrigerator. My glorious storehouse."

The pengbot pointed to a small doorway

in the far wall. Through the door the penguins could see a huge aquarium of fish swimming around.

"Fresh fish all day, every day," said Dark Wader. "My RoboSeals load them into the vending machines you see all over the *Death Starfish*. No more tasteless alien life forms. This is the real thing."

"Sardines. Mullet. Mackerel," sighed Rocky, gazing at the aquarium. "All my favorite kinds. The *Tunafish* ran out of those years ago."

Captain Krill looked at his crew. If penguins had lips, they would have been licking them. He hoped they weren't falling for Beaky's smooth talk. He needed them to stay focused. "Where did you get them, Wader?" he asked.

"I swiped a few from the *Tunafish* freezer when I left," said Dark Wader.

"*What?*" roared Fuzz.

Dark Wader shrugged. "I only needed a few species. I cloned them — I know, I'm a genius. Now I have as much fish as I want."

"You're nothing but a mullet thief!" shouted Fuzz. "A sardine pirate! A mackerel pickpocket!"

"Can it, Fuzz," said Captain Krill sharply, before his security officer had them all turned into fish food. "What do you want from us, Wader?"

Dark Wader smirked. "I'm building a penguin paradise so I can rule the universe in comfort. But it's lonely being the only penguin here. I want you all to join me. Permanently."

The Space Penguins blinked in surprise.

"I was going to get in touch when I finished this place," Dark Wader went on. "But then you turned up uninvited, so I've decided to ask you now. Imagine it! We can recreate all of our best days on the *Tunafish*. We had fun, didn't we? Who remembers the day I ran engine oil through the plumbing and nearly wrecked Krill's waterproof feathers when he was taking a shower? Happy times!"

"You've got a funny idea of happy times," said Captain Krill.

"If you stay here with me, you'll have all the snow you want," the big pengbot said.

"All the best rocks for nesting. Fish all day, every day. No more rattling through space in that old heap of fish-shaped junk. And the ice slides . . ." He paused temptingly. "There are ice slides in this place you wouldn't believe. We could live in comfort and companionship, and rule the universe together. What do you say?"

"Could we maybe try another ice slide before deciding, Captain?" Rocky asked hopefully. "And a couple of mullet sandwiches?"

"We want to know where the *Doughball's* pilot is," Captain Krill said with determination. "We demand that you release him and his spacecraft, and then we want to leave. We don't want to rule the universe. We want to protect it. It needs us."

"I need you too!" pleaded Dark Wader. "I'm *lonely*!"

"Sorry," said Captain Krill. "But that's our final decision."

The pengbot looked utterly furious. "Oh, poo!" he said. "Then you'll all have to die instead." He turned to his RoboSeals. "Take them away!"

CHAPTER EIGHT

SHELLFISH ESCAPE

The jail cells were right next door to the sleeping pods in Point Two, but they couldn't have been more different. The Space Penguins' cell had three walls of steel and one wall of bars, plus a large door with a huge steel padlock.

"We have to get out of here!" Fuzz shouted, rattling the bars. "Who does that metal moon loon think he is?"

Rocky waddled back and forth in the cell, his eyebrows bobbing. "What if . . ." he began. "No, scrap that. How about . . . oh, no way. Why —"

Just at that moment, a strange yellow creature crept into view from a dark corner of the cell. It waved three of its six arms.

"Um, hello?" it said, sounding excited. "I'm Bobby Cheese. Pilot of the *Doughball*, the fastest pizza-delivery ship in Section D of the universe. Are you the intergalactic heroes of the *Tunafish*?"

The penguins looked at each other.

"That's us," said Splash.

Bobby Cheese started stuttering. "Oh, w-w-wow! I can't believe you came! I'm honored!" He shook the penguins' flippers so hard that their blubbery parts started wobbling. With so many arms, shaking all their flippers took no time at all.

"So what's the rescue plan?" Bobby Cheese asked eagerly.

"We're working on something right now, Cheese," Captain Krill assured him. "Aren't we, crew?"

"I'm considering strategies," said Fuzz.

"I'm considering strategies too," said Rocky.

Which basically meant neither Fuzz nor Rocky had a rescue plan yet.

"Splash?" said Captain Krill.

Splash smiled. "Naturally, I have a solution to our dilemma, Captain."

He lifted his plump white belly with both flippers and revealed a small egg-shaped toolbox nestled on top of his feet.

"Oh happy haddock!" said Fuzz. "We've slid. We've swum. We've danced through falling icicles. We've avoided the steel jaws of a robot killer whale, and we've wound up in jail. And all that time you've kept a toolbox balanced on your feet! You'd make one heck of a dad!"

"I took the precaution of gluing this toolbox into place shortly before the RoboSeals broke down the door of the *Tunafish*," said Splash. He rummaged inside the box and produced a small pair of pliers and a pile of prawn shells. "I took the prawn shells while we were having breakfast," he added. "You never know when things might be useful. Stand aside now. Things could get fishy."

Splash's flippers worked in a blur of flashing steel and prawn pieces.

"Ta-da," he said with a final flourish of the pliers. "One shellfish skeleton key. Guaranteed to open anything."

It was miraculous! It was perfect! It was orange and slightly stinky!

Fuzz snatched the key from Splash and inserted it into the padlock. The cell door flew open. At once, the little jellyfish-cam, which had slid into the jail cell a short distance behind the penguins, alerted the control room.

BREAKOUT, it transmitted. The screen in the control room flashed in big red letters: BREAKOUT.

The *Death Starfish*'s alarm system kicked into action. The walls flashed with warning lights and alarms ripped through the air, deafening the penguins.

WHOOPWHOOPWHOOP!

"This way!" Captain Krill shouted, spotting a hole carved into the icy wall

outside the cell. It was too dark to read
where it led.

They hurtled down the tunnel. Each
time they approached a fork, steel doors
slammed shut and forced them to change
direction. Captain Krill had a nasty feeling
they were being herded.

At last they shot into the air and crashed,
beak-first, into a familiar-looking snowdrift.
The jellyfish-cam landed in the drift behind
Captain Krill with a muffled plop.

Crabba snapped his claws in front of them. Masher and Cruncher snarled. The army of RoboSeals clapped their metal flippers, and the penguins heard the familiar sound of falling icicles. *Ching.*

They were back on the Great Ice Deck.

"*Ice* of you to drop in," said Dark Wader.

"You used that joke already, Wader," said Rocky.

"I told you I was good at recycling," said the pengbot.

There was only one thing to do.

"Waddle for your lives, crew!" shouted Captain Krill. "Follow me!"

They bolted. The ranks of RoboSeals raced after them, red eyes glowing. They were faster than they looked. At times like this, Captain Krill wished he had a set of wheels like Dark Wader's.

The RoboSeals were closing in. "Do you have anything useful in your toolbox, Splash?" Captain Krill shouted.

Splash pulled out a flask of sloshing purple liquid from his toolbox. "This might do the trick!" he shouted.

He opened the flask and emptied it onto the ice. A familiar sock-like smell assaulted the penguins' nostrils. There were a series

of loud bangs and fizzes behind them. The RoboSeals had touched the stinky gunk and started exploding.

"I analyzed the corrosive properties of the purple blobs shortly after we left the planet Tentakle," Splash explained breathlessly. "Then I recreated it in liquid form. The battle with the RoboSeals at the *Tunafish* showed me that it might prove useful."

Captain Krill could feel the hot metal breath of the surviving RoboSeals on the back of his tail. Splash's blob-bomb had slowed them down, but not by much.

"Got any more?" he asked.

"Nope," said Splash.

"Looks like we'll just have to go a little faster then," said Rocky.

"Stop waddling and give up!" roared Dark Wader.

"Never!" Fuzz shouted back, struggling to keep up with the others on his short legs.

An ice hole in the ground marked SPACEPORT loomed into view.

"Head for that hole!" Captain Krill yelled.

The little jellyfish-cam leaped onto Rocky's belt as Rocky and Splash jumped down the hole first. Captain Krill gave Bobby Cheese a brisk shove in the back. But as he leaped after the pizza commander, the captain heard something behind him that made him groan.

"Take *that*, you ridiculous rustbucket! You bionic bilge pump! And that! And that! No one chases Fuzz Allgrin and lives to tell the tale!"

CHAPTER NINE

CHEESEBALLS AND FISH CANNONS

The penguins landed with a whump on the ice beside the gleaming spaceport where they'd first arrived. There was not a single RoboSeal in sight. The landing bays and shiny Squid-G fighters were quiet.

Rocky suddenly noticed the jellyfish-cam on his belt. He knocked it off in disgust. "Ugh," he said. "I picked up something icky. I hate to think where it's been."

The jellyfish-cam skidded across the icy ground toward the *Tunafish*.

"Where's Fuzz?" asked Rocky, looking around.

"Fuzz stayed back to fight," Captain Krill said grimly.

"Is he crazy?" exclaimed Bobby Cheese. "He's no bigger than an anchovy!"

"You should be glad Fuzz isn't here, Cheese," Splash said. "He'd grill you for that."

"Then you'd be toasted Cheese," Rocky added.

The pizza commander gawked at the spectacular spacecraft parked in the cargo bay in front of the *Tunafish*.

"That's my ship!" he squeaked. "What have they done to it? It's amazing!"

The *Doughball*'s rust was gone. Tentacles of steel sprouted from its tail. A sharp beak-like nose stuck out at the front. Bright new engines glittered on its belly.

Rocky whistled. "They've turned your rustbucket into a Squid-G fighter, Cheese!"

Captain Krill clapped his flippers under Rocky's beak. "Concentrate, Rocky! We have to go back and rescue Fuzz before Wader sends his RoboSeals after us!"

"We'll have to use our strengths," said Splash. "Where are we at our fastest and most unstoppable?"

"Somewhere without RoboSeals," said Rocky.

Captain Krill slapped his forehead with a flipper. "Of course! Somewhere we can swim!"

"I hate to point it out, but this place is no Antarctic Ocean," said Rocky.

"We need zero gravity, not water!" Captain Krill said. "In zero gravity we can swim at incredible speeds. We were designed for it."

Splash smiled. "And when Beaky rebuilt himself as a robot, I bet he lost the ability to swim in zero gravity," he added. "You've seen how well he moves on land with those wheels. I don't think you can have it both ways."

Captain Krill nodded. "That's right. So in zero gravity . . ."

"Wader's toast!" whooped Rocky.

"Now all we have to do is find the mechanism that controls the gravity on this space station and switch it off," said the captain. "Right, Splash?"

"One hundred percent correct, Captain," replied Splash. He pointed at an ice hole carved into the opposite wall. The sign said CONTROL ROOM. "And there's a good place to start looking."

"Rocky?" said Captain Krill. "We need your speed through these ice tunnels if we're going to find and disable the gravity system before Wader catches up with us. Cheese can go with you. Three extra pairs of arms could come in handy."

"Um," said Bobby Cheese. He backed toward the refurbished *Doughball*. "I think you're great, and I can't thank you enough and everything. Unfortunately, anti-gravity missions and fights with weird penguin robots and their metal seals just aren't really my thing. In fact, I need to be going. I have pizzas to deliver."

"But we need your arms!" Captain Krill said. "You have so many of them and —"

But Bobby Cheese had already reached the new-looking *Doughball* and was swinging himself into the driver's seat. "I'm rechristening my ship the *Cheeseball*!" he shouted. "Sorry, but I really have to go. Whenever you want pizzas, just give me a call. I'll give you ten percent off your order!"

The gleaming *Cheeseball*'s engine roared smoothly to life, filling the cargo bay with the smell of old sardine oil.

"Ten percent off?" said Rocky in disgust. "His distress call said we could have them for free!"

"We're wasting time," said the captain. "Fuzz needs us. Can you find the gravity system and turn it off by yourself, Rocky?"

"Leave it to me, Captain!"

"Get to the Fish Station as soon as your

mission is complete. Splash and I will meet you there. We need all flippers on full."

Rocky leaped into the control room ice tunnel just as a set of vast steel doors sealed them off from the spaceport and the *Cheeseball* blasted away.

"Are you sure you did the right thing by sending Rocky, Captain?" said Splash. "His sense of direction isn't entirely reliable."

"I thought about sending you instead, Splash," said the captain, "but I need you for something else. Follow me. We have to find a tunnel to the Fish Station."

Thousands of fish swam through huge glass tanks above and around Splash and the captain. Their scales flashed and gleamed in the icy light. The two Space Penguins could hear Dark Wader shouting at his RoboSeals in the next room.

"What do you mean, you can't find them? Look *harder*!"

Splash dusted himself down after an extra-speedy ride through the *Death Starfish* tunnels. "Now what?"

"Come on then, you corrugated cake pan!" came Fuzz's enraged voice. "Take a bite!"

Through the connecting door to the Great
Ice Deck, Captain Krill and Splash caught
sight of Fuzz. He was dangling in a cage
over the water tank, kicking and punching
at the bars. With a creak and a lurch, the
cage dropped a little lower.

"Wader's feeding Fuzz to the whale!" cried Captain Krill, rushing toward the connecting door for a closer look. One waddling foot caught the edge of a nearby fish vending machine.

CCCLLLAAANNNGGG!

"OW!"

Hundreds of red RoboSeal eyes swiveled to face Captain Krill as he hopped about in the doorway.

"Don't worry about me, Captain!" yelled Fuzz. "That briny barnacled banana doesn't stand a chance against the Fuzzmeister!" He flung himself at the bars of his cage and gnawed at them like an angry hamster.

"We have unfortunately lost our element of surprise," said Splash.

"Get them!" roared Dark Wader.

RoboSeals raced toward them. Captain Krill tried to close the Fish Station door. It wouldn't budge.

"Here's the plan," said the captain. "We'll have to act a little faster than I had hoped, but we should still be okay. I'm going to jam the button on this vending machine. Then you can help me move the machine so that it blocks the door, face out. We'll need your toolbox, Splash."

"Faster, you mechanized mud flaps!" Dark Wader screamed at the RoboSeals.

The penguins heaved the vending machine until it sat snugly in the doorway. They could hear the sound of mackerel hitting the Great Ice Deck on the other side. *PING. PING. PING.*

"Can you make the mechanism throw fish out any faster?" said Captain Krill.

"How fast do you want?" asked Splash.

"What's the fastest speed you can think of?" said Captain Krill.

"Light moves at one hundred eighty-six thousand miles per second," Splash replied.

"Maybe not that fast," said Captain Krill. "But do your best."

Splash whipped off the back of the machine and started tinkering with the mechanism. Captain Krill could see the cogs and wheels speeding up, turning faster and faster. *PING*, went the mackerel. Then *PING PING*.

Then *PING-PING-PING-PING-PING* . . .

Through the tiny gap between the edge of their new fish cannon and the doorframe, Captain Krill watched the RoboSeals. They lurched about in confusion as the fishy missiles battered into them.

The cage dropped farther. Fuzz's shrieks of rage grew louder. "Gimme all you've got, blubberchops!"

Captain Krill and Splash exchanged worried looks.

"Where's Rocky?" said the captain. "We're running out of time!"

And then time ran out completely as the great robot whale leaped up toward Fuzz with its jaws gaping wide.

CHAPTER TEN

ONE FOR ALL AND ALL FOR FISH

Somewhere in the middle of the *Death Starfish*, Rocky hurtled along with his eyebrows flowing behind him like streamers. He'd got lost three times already, but at least he was getting faster with every tunnel he tried.

Zooming out of the fourth and final tunnel at forty miles an hour, he hit a massive wall of flashing buttons feet-first.

WHEEPWHEEPWARPWARPWAAARPP went

the buttons. Half of them
dropped out of the control
wall and hit the floor in
a tangle of wires. Three
LED lights exploded.

"Whoops!" Rocky
waved at the three
stunned-looking RoboSeals
beside the broken control panel. "Is this the
control room?"

A RoboSeal gave a menacing nod.

"Did I hit the anti-gravity button?"

The nodding RoboSeal lunged at him
with a snarl. It only got halfway when its
butt lifted off the ground and floated up
toward the ceiling, making the RoboSeal do
a clumsy somersault in midair. The other
two joined it with surprised expressions on
their gleaming silver faces.

"Looks like I did," said Rocky as his body
lifted off the ground as well.

Angling his flippers, he made a quick turn in midair. He spotted an ice hole marked FISH STATION just behind the nearest upside down RoboSeal.

"Gotta go," he said with a wave. "Sorry to leave you hanging!"

And Rocky zoomed away down the tunnel to find the others

With a small but powerful kick, Captain Krill shot sideways through the Fish Station with a whoop.

"Zero gravity!" he shouted happily. "Rocky did it!"

Splash and Captain Krill rocketed around the room a couple of times to test their speed, dodging the peculiar blobs of water rising from the Fish Station tanks and carrying a bunch of confused-looking fish. Then Rocky zoomed out of the Fish Station ice tunnel and almost smashed into Splash.

"Sorry it took a while," he said, pushing his eyebrows out of the way. "What did I miss?"

"Me, you idiot," Splash shouted. "Barely."

The fish cannon vending machine had lifted off the ground now, opening up the blocked door. Light from the Great Ice Deck flooded into the Fish Station, together with at least twenty RoboSeals. Half of them were flying for the first time in their lives. They looked a little upset about it.

Captain Krill spun around and pointed his beak at the gaping door. "Time to get Fuzz out of that cage!" he said.

The three penguin astronauts dodged the floating RoboSeals and hurtled onto the Great Ice Deck. Dollops of water from the great tank floated around the cave like overblown soap bubbles. Glittering icicles hung in midair, spinning gently. RoboSeals were doing somersaults and attacking each other in confusion.

"I'm over here," shouted Rocky, zooming past an angry robot. "Now I'm over *here*! Can't catch me!"

Dark Wader floated past, upside down. There was an ominous crack as the back of his armor smashed against the icy wall.

"*Crabba!*" he screamed. "I think I'm broken!"

Captain Krill expertly zigzagged through the tumbling RoboSeals toward Fuzz's cage as it spun in slow circles. The robot whale was now rising from what was left of the tank. Water rolled off his enormous body in all directions. A big glob floated straight through the fresh crack in the back of Dark Wader's armor.

"CRABBAAAA! I've got a wet butt! Hurry up before I short-circuit!" Dark Wader roared.

"Coming, boss!" squealed Crabba from up near the ceiling.

By flicking its huge tail, the whale had some kind of control in the air. Its red eyes gleamed as it swam toward Fuzz. Captain Krill surged at Fuzz's cage with a webbed kick.

His beak slammed into the cage like a
power-driven chisel. The cage exploded in
slow motion.

"Yippee!" shouted Fuzz. He danced on
the whale's black metal nose and launched
himself skyward. "Come and get me now,
you great greasy glob!" he yelled.

Captain Krill felt the snap of a tumbling RoboSeal's jaws brush a little too close to his tail. He grabbed a mackerel bullet from the fish cannon as it floated past and lobbed it at the snapping monster. The mackerel flew up one the robot's metal nostrils. The RoboSeal blew up with a loud *BANG*.

"Come to mama!" Fuzz shouted at the angry whale. He flung an armful of mackerel as hard as he could. "Wham, blam, mackerel jam!"

Dark Wader was sizzling like a frying pan on the far side of the Great Ice Deck. His waterproof armor was ruined. Dancing blobs of water from the whale tank were making their way into his suit and wreaking havoc with his circuitry.

"I thought . . . *bbzzt* . . . that little jellyfish spy thing you sent after Krill and his cronies was supposed to . . . *zstz* . . . warn us about this kind of thing, Crabba," Dark Wader hissed. "We haven't heard a . . . *zxzx* . . . thing since the jail break!"

Crabba hurriedly tried to fix the wet electrics sparking out of his boss's armored chest. "It was a prototype," replied Crabba. "Prototypes are always unreliable. Stay still, boss, or you'll be eating fried crab for dinner."

Rocky and Splash joined the fish-hurling. *PING . . . PING . . . PING . . .* The mackerel moved much slower in zero gravity, but they were effective just the same. *BANG! BANG! BANG!* The penguins blew up three more RoboSeals, including the gigantic Masher. Shattered robot components and broken metal teeth twirled around the room.

"WAHOO!" yelled Rocky as Cruncher exploded extra loudly.

"NOOO—*bzsyst*—OOO!" howled Dark Wader.

"Time to go," Captain Krill said.

"They're escaping. . . *ping . . . pziznzg!*"
shouted Dark Wader. His
helmet started smoking.
"Fetch, Cyril! *Fetch!*"

The whale's eyes blazed.
It beat its tail extra hard.
For such a large creature,
it moved very fast.

"The whale's name is Cyril?" said Rocky.
"I almost feel sorry for it now."

"You pathetic mechanized mussel —"
Fuzz began. He spun back to face the
charging whale, just as the penguins
reached the spaceport ice hole. Fuzz was
holding a fresh pile of fish bullets in his
flippers.

"Oh no you don't," said Rocky, shoving
Fuzz into the tunnel.

SMASH!

The ice tunnel went black as the whale
plunged after them. The tunnel heaved and

shuddered, throwing Captain Krill against the walls.

"I think Cyril just got stuck!" Rocky shouted.

There was an awful grinding sound behind them. Cyril had wedged himself tight. The tunnel rang with his enraged bellowing.

"That's good news, crew," Captain Krill said, righting himself. "Wader can't follow us now. Onward and outward!"

They zoomed into the great white spaceport. The *Tunafish* waited for them in midair.

"No Squid-G makeover for you, babe," said Rocky glumly, looking at the *Tunafish*'s rusty patches. "Though at least they fixed the hole Fuzz made with the bazooka-blaster and put the door back on. I guess they didn't have time to do the rest."

"Where did the pizza guy go?" asked Fuzz, looking around for the *Doughball*.

Captain Krill darted through the door of the *Tunafish*. "Delivering out-of-space pizzas a whole lot faster, Fuzz," replied Krill. "We got him out. Our mission here is complete."

"Welcome back," said ICEcube. "I was starting to feel lonely — and computers never feel lonely."

"It's good to be back, ICEcube," said Rocky, preparing to start the engine. "Hit the exit button on your way aboard, Splash!"

"Your fish is my command!" Splash shouted back.

"Did Splash just make a joke?" said Fuzz, rocketing into the ship with his flippers full of mackerel.

"It does occasionally happen," said Splash, zooming in after him.

"Get the dinner on, Fuzz," said Captain Krill, rubbing his flippers. "I fancy mackerel tonight."

Steel doors slammed into place, sealing off the spaceport from the rest of the *Death Starfish*. The space station's massive external doors heaved open. With a roar of its engines, the *Tunafish* lifted off and zoomed out into the blackness. Captain Krill's faint shout echoed through the silent stars.

"Good to see you again, universe! The *Tunafish* is back on the case!"

P.S.

Fixed firmly on the underside of the *Tunafish*, where it had been since Rocky had flicked it off his belt, the little jellyfish-cam sent a little message back through a million light-years of Deep Space.

ON BOARD THE *TUNAFISH*. MESSAGES TO FOLLOW.

"The jellyfish-cam!" Crabba exclaimed. He looked up from the workbench where he was repairing Dark Wader's armor. Parts of RoboSeal and broken pieces of the robot whale lay nearby. "It's working after all!"

"Prepare for payback, Crabba," growled the half-naked pengbot, shivering on his commander's chair. "Next time I meet Krill and his crew, I will not show them any mercy. I will not give them any second chances. And I will most definitely not give them any pizza."

ABOUT THE AUTHOR

LUCY COURTENAY has been writing children's fiction for a long time. She's written for book series like The Sleepover Club, Animal Ark, Dolphin Diaries, Beast Quest, Naughty Fairies, Dream Dogs, Animal Antics, Scarlet Silver, Wild, and Space Penguins. Additionally, her desk drawers are filled with half-finished stories waiting for the right moment to emerge and dance around. In her spare time, she sings with assorted choirs and forages for mushrooms (which her husband wisely refuses to eat).

ABOUT THE ILLUSTRATOR

JAMES DAVIES is a London-based illustrator, author, and pro-wrestling expert who grew up in the 1980s and loved to draw video-game bad guys and dig in the garden for dinosaur bones. Since then, James has gone to college, gotten a haircut or two, and is extremely busy working on all kinds of book projects.

GLOSSARY

BOAST (BOHST)—to brag or talk about something in order to impress others

CORROSIVE (kuh-ROH-siv)—having the ability to burn or melt things

DISTRESS (di-STRESS)—to be in danger and really need help

EXTERNAL (ek-STUR-nuhl)—being on the outside

FUSELAGE (FYOO-suh-lahzh)—the main part of an aircraft that holds the passengers, crew, and cargo

MISSION (MISH-uhn)—an important job that someone told you to do

OMINOUS (AH-muh-nuhss)—giving the feeling that something bad will happen or something is not right

PRECAUTION (pri-KAW-shuhn)—something you do ahead of time in order to make sure things work out well or to make sure nothing bad happens

PREDATOR (PRED-uh-ter)—an animal that hunts and eats other animals in order to live

PROTOTYPE (PROH-tuh-tipe)—the first version of an invention used as a test to see if the idea works

REFURBISH (ri-FUR-bish)—to make something like new again

STRATEGY (STRAT-i-jee)—a carefully thought-out plan

DISCUSSION QUESTIONS

1. Why do you think Dark Wader originally left the Space Penguins? Talk about some possible reasons.

2. What kind of training do you think the Space Penguins went through to become astronauts? Would you want to train to be an astronaut?

3. Dark Wader tried to build the perfect home for penguins. What would your dream home look like?

WRITING PROMPTS

1. Write a story about what happened after Dark Wader left the Space Penguins. How did Beaky Wader become the pengbot known as Dark Wader?

2. Which Space Penguin is your favorite? List reasons why he's your favorite, and use examples from the book.

3. The Space Penguins could have stayed at the space station where they had fun ice slides and yummy food, but they decided not to stay with Dark Wader. Write a paragraph about what you would have done.